CL 16

SL(

2

For Sarah
C.C.

To Bobbie Lee, with love xx
J.McC.

Reading Consultant: Prue Goodwin, Lecturer in literacy and children's books

ORCHARD BOOKS
338 Euston Road, London NW1 3BH
Orchard Books Australia
Hachette Children's Books
Level 17/207 Kent Street, Sydney NSW 2000

First published in 2011 by Orchard Books
First paperback publication in 2012

Text © Catherine Coe 2011
Illustrations © Jan McCafferty 2011

ISBN 978 1 40830 690 1 (hardback)
ISBN 978 1 40830 698 7 (paperback)

The rights of Catherine Coe to be identified as the author and
Jan McCafferty to be identified as the illustrator of this work
have been asserted by them in accordance with the
Copyright, Designs and Patents Act, 1988.

1 3 5 7 9 10 8 6 4 2   (hardback)
1 3 5 7 9 10 8 6 4 2   (paperback)

Printed in China

Orchard Books is a division of Hachette Children's Books,
an Hachette UK company.

www.hachette.co.uk

Rocky Rodeo

Written by
Catherine Coe **Illustrated by**
Jan McCafferty

ORCHARD

The Rocky Rodeo funfair was coming to town. Casper the Kid Cowboy couldn't wait to go on all the rides!

"There's the Big Wheel and the Runaway Train rollercoaster and the Ultimate Loop-the-loop!" Casper told his best friend, Pete, as they sat beside their treehouse hide-out.

PRIVATE!

KEEP OUT

Pete looked worried. He didn't really like funfair rides, especially rollercoasters. He was afraid of heights. But Pete didn't say anything. He didn't want Casper to think he was silly.

Soon it was the day of the funfair. Pete was *very* nervous. He hoped Casper might have changed his mind about going.

But Casper arrived at Pete's ranch early. He didn't want to miss a minute of the fair!

Casper was wearing his best
red cowboy boots.

His horse, Blue the Brave, was
dressed up too!

Pete had felt too worried to get dressed properly.

"I don't feel very well," Pete said. But Casper had already galloped off.

There were lots of signs for
the funfair on the way.
"It's going to be mighty fine!"
Casper said.

But the signs made Pete feel
a whole lot worse . . .

ROCKY RODEO
FUNFAIR!
Get ready for
THRILLS and
spills!

Are you brave
enough for the
Rocky
Rodeo?

Next stop:
non-stop
rocky rides!

By the time the two cowboys
got there, Pete looked quite ill.
"I feel a bit sick," he said
to Casper.

But Casper was already running towards the Big Wheel. And Pete didn't want to let his best friend down.

Pete held on tight while the
Big Wheel circled round.
"Yee-ha!" Casper cried, waving
his arms. He looked very happy.
Pete couldn't wait for it to
be over.

"That was brilliant!" Casper
shouted as they got off. "Let's
go on a bigger one!"

Casper ran over to the Runaway
Train rollercoaster. Pete thought
it looked very . . . twisty!
"I might not go on this one,"
Pete said.

But Casper didn't hear him.
He pulled Pete into some
empty seats.

The ride started. It was very fast, and went up and down and round and round. Pete looked very green.

As the Runaway Train came to a stop, Pete was sick – all over Casper!

But Casper was too excited to be worried about his dirty clothes, or even about his best friend. He wanted to go faster and higher!

Casper saw the Ultimate
Loop-the-loop up ahead. "Yee-ha!"
he said. "That looks *amazing*!"

Pete looked up . . . and up . . .
and up. It was the highest ride
he'd ever seen – and it went
upside-down!
"Casper, that looks too high
for me," Pete said. "I'll wait here."
Casper *still* didn't hear him.
"Come on, Pete!" he called.

Pete followed Casper to the entrance. But the man in charge was shaking his head. They were too small to go on the ride!

Pete was *very* relieved.
Casper was *very* disappointed.

Suddenly, Pete had a bright
idea to cheer Casper up.
"We can build a funfair of
our own!" he said. "Just wait
and see!"

Back at his ranch, Pete put his plan into action. Casper soon saw what his best friend was doing and joined in.

"I didn't really like the rides at the Rocky Rodeo funfair," Pete admitted. "Our rides are much better!"

"Didn't you?" Casper said, surprised. But he could see that Pete was much happier now.

The best friends had so much
fun at their own funfair.
No one told them they were too
small – and none of the rides
made Pete sick!

Yee-ha!

Even their horses joined in!

As the sun went down, Casper and Pete ate candyfloss and popcorn in their treehouse hide-out.

"I was too excited about the Rocky Rodeo funfair to listen to you," Casper said to Pete. "I'm sorry."

"It's OK," Pete said. He could see his best friend felt bad. "And we had a mighty fine time at our own funfair!"

Casper smiled. "We sure did, partner!" he said.

Written by
Catherine Coe

Illustrated by
Jan McCafferty

All priced at £8.99

Orchard Books are available from all good bookshops,
or can be ordered from our website: www.orchardbooks.co.uk,
or telephone 01235 827702, or fax 01235 827703.

Prices and availability are subject to change.